The Great Lemonade Stand Standoff

Read all the books in The Secret Slide
Money Club series!

The Great Lemonade Stand Standoff

The Mad Cash Dash

Trouble at the Toy Store

The Secret Slide $ Money Club series

The Great Lemonade Stand Standoff

Art Rainer

B&H kids
Nashville TN

Published by B&H Publishing Group
Nashville, Tennessee

Dewey Decimal Classification: JF
Subject Heading: PERSONAL FINANCE / MONEY-MAKING
PROJECTS FOR CHILDREN / STEWARDSHIP

1 2 3 4 5 6 7 • 22 21 20 19

To my sons—Nathaniel,
Joshua, and James

Contents

Introduction

This is the story about three fun, smart, and crazy kids who have one big challenge—to rescue people from a mean and selfish villain named Albatross. (Say it with me: *AL-ba-tross.*)

Well, the kids don't know about their big challenge yet. But they will soon. (Please don't tell them about it now. It will ruin the surprise.)

Jake, Sophia, and Brody are three awesome kids. Let me tell you about them.

Jake loves adventure and is very competitive. He plays drums and can dribble a basketball between his legs. But he does get in trouble sometimes, mostly because he talks too much and can't seem to stay still.

Sophia is all about school and learning. She respects others and always makes the highest grade in her class. Sophia plays the violin and can finish a 1,000-piece puzzle in a week. But she does not like risks, which can be a problem if you need to rescue people from a villain.

Brody is a fun and crazy kid. He has a great imagination. Brody plays the guitar and has high score on *Planet Blaster*. But sometimes he can lose track of time and be late.

Now you know about Jake, Sophia, and Brody, who are about to discover the Secret Slide Money Club.

(Please don't tell them that either.)

Chapter 1
Something Stinks

It was Friday, and school was almost over. Jake, Sophia, and Brody were sitting at their desks.

Brody leaned over to Jake's desk and whispered, "Hey, Drew has been sad all day. Do you know why?"

"I have no clue," whispered Jake. "At lunch, I asked him if he wanted some of my pizza. He said no. Who turns down pizza?"

"That is weird. Do you have any pizza left? I'll eat it."

"No! Lunch ended three hours ago."

"I know. It's sad. I miss lunch," Brody said.

Jake smiled at Brody.

Sophia was sitting in front of the boys. "Be quiet, you guys! I can't hear Ms. Warren," she said.

Ms. Warren stopped teaching "Sophia? Is there something you would like to share?"

Sophia was embarrassed. Her face turned red. "No, ma'am," she said. She looked back at Jake and Brody with an angry face. Brody snickered.

Jake leaned over to Brody. "Did you see Drew at recess?" he whispered.

"I did," Brody said. "He just sat by the fence. He didn't play with anybody."

"That's not like Drew," Jake said. "Something must be wrong."

Sophia turned around again. She put her finger on her lips. "Shhhhhh!"

Again, Ms. Warren heard Sophia and stopped teaching. "Sophia, can you please be quiet? You are distracting those around you."

Jake and Brody looked at Ms. Warren. "Thank you, Ms. Warren," they said together.

Sophia turned red again. She never got in trouble. Now she was in trouble twice in just a few minutes!

Jake and Brody both snickered.

Sophia looked back at the boys and gave them another angry face.

Just then, the bell rang. The school week was over. Hello, weekend!

Ms. Warren spoke. "Don't forget that Monday is the last day to turn in money for the pet-shelter fund-raiser. We're giving money to help lost or hurt animals. And we only need twenty dollars to reach our class goal!"

Sophia took out her notebook and wrote:

Need $20 for goal

She always kept good notes. She got up from her desk and walked back to Jake and Brody.

"Why did you do that to me?" she asked.

"That's what best friends are for!" Brody said.

Sophia rolled her eyes. "Whatever," she said.

"Sophia, did you notice how Drew was sad all day?" Jake said. "He didn't even want to try my pizza at lunch. Who doesn't want pizza?"

"You know, he was really quiet at his locker too," Sophia said.

Jake and Sophia looked at Brody. He was chewing something.

"What's in your mouth?" asked Sophia.

"Gum," replied Brody.

Jake and Sophia looked at each other. Then they looked back at Brody.

"And where did you get that gum?" asked Jake.

"Oh, I found it stuck under my desk today," Brody said. "I have been waiting all day to chew it. It's strawberry flavored!"

"EWWWW!" Sophia said. "That's gross!"

"What? You don't like strawberry gum?" asked Brody.

"We like strawberry gum," Jake said. "We don't like old, used strawberry gum!"

Brody blew a bubble with his gum and popped it. He smiled.

"Yuck!" Sophia said.

"Well, I like it," Brody said. "It may be old and used, but it is still good!"

"Hey, do you want to meet at the playground tomorrow morning?" Jake asked.

"Sure," Sophia said.

Brody blew another bubble and popped it. "I'll see you there," he said.

Sophia rolled her eyes again. "That gum is so gross."

Brody smiled.

"Are you going to give money to help the pet shelter?" asked Sophia.

The boys laughed. "Nope!" Jake said. "We spent most of our money on toys and snacks."

"I guess I won't either," Sophia said.

Just then, the three friends smelled something stinky.

"What is that smell?" Sophia asked.

"I don't know," Brody said. "But it's awful!"

They held their noses and left the classroom. The school week was over, but the adventure was about to begin.

Chapter 2
The Secret Slide

The next day, Jake and Sophia waited for Brody at the Oak City Park playground.

"Where could he be?" asked Sophia.

"Who knows?" Jake said.

Just then, they saw Brody running down the street toward the playground.

"Here he comes," Sophia said. "It's about time."

"What took you so long?" Jake asked.

"Cereal," Brody said.

"Cereal?" asked Sophia.

"Yes, cereal," Brody said. "We had a new box of Chocolate Rock Starz. It was amazing! I had three bowls."

"That was a lot of cereal," Jake said.

"It was. My stomach hurts a little, but it was worth it!" Brody said.

"Yuck," Sophia said.

Brody held his nose. "Hey, you both stink!"

"No, you stink!" Jake said.

"That's the same stink that stunk yesterday!" Sophia said. "Maybe it really *is* us!"

"Look up there!" Jake pointed to the deck, next to the top of the spiral tube slide. A green glow was coming from what looked like a small door.

The three friends hurried up to the deck. But the glowing stopped.

"What happened?" asked Jake.

Jake put his hand on the little door. It started glowing green again.

"Look out!" Sophia said.

The three jumped back. The door opened!

"You broke it!" Brody said.

"No I didn't!" Jake said.

The three stared at what the door had been hiding . . . a control panel with three buttons. Above each button was a word.

Sophia read the words, "GIVE, SAVE, LIVE."

"Wow! What do you think it means?" asked Brody.

Jake pushed the LIVE button.

ERRRRRRRR!!! The control panel made a loud noise and glowed red.

He tried the SAVE button.

ERRRRRRRR!!!

That did not work either. Then Jake tried the GIVE button.

DING!!!

But nothing else happened.

"Maybe there is a pattern," Sophia said. "Now try the LIVE button."

Jake did.

ERRRRRRRR!!!

"Try the SAVE button," Sophia said.

DING!!!

"GIVE—SAVE—LIVE must be the pattern," Sophia said.

Jake pressed the LIVE button.

DING!!! DING!!! DING!!!

The tube slide next to the door started glowing bright green.

"Um, I guess it liked that pattern," Brody said.

Sophia took out her notebook and wrote,

Give—Save—Live

"Come on! Let's go down the slide!" yelled Jake.

"I don't know about that . . . ," Sophia said.

"Well, I'm going!" said Jake. He threw himself down the slide. "WEEEEEEE!"

"Me too!" yelled Brody. "YEAAAAAAH!"

Sophia watched Brody disappear down the slide. The boys' yells got farther away.

"Ugh," she said. "Okay. Here I go. WOOOAAAAH!"

It was a bumpy ride. Sophia heard the boys cheering ahead of her. Then she rolled out of the slide.

The boys sat on the ground, staring, mouths open. They were in an underground

headquarters. Buttons and screens were everywhere.

"Whoa!" Jake stood up. "This place is awesome." He brushed himself off . . . and noticed their clothing. Black suits. Green ties. And really cool sunglasses. "What—?" He pointed at his friends.

"I don't know if we should be here." Sophia slipped her sunglasses off and looked at them more closely.

"Look at that!" Jake said. He pointed at a car with rockets on the back.

Jake and Sophia noticed that Brody did not say anything. They looked at Brody and started laughing.

"It's not funny," Brody said.

Brody's tie was not around his neck—it was on his head!

"I think the slide is broken," Brody said.

Sophia laughed. "I think the slide works just fine!"

Then they heard a voice.

"Welcome to the Secret Slide Money Club!"

Chapter 3

Welcome to the Club!

The voice made Jake, Sophia, and Brody jump.

"Who are you?" Jake yelled.

Sophia spun around. "And where are you?" she asked.

One of the screens on the wall lit up. On the screen was a guy wearing a suit, a tie, and really cool sunglasses, just like them. He had a friendly smile.

"I did not mean to scare you," said the man. "My name is Agent G.B."

Jake, Sophia, and Brody turned toward the screen.

"What do you want from us?" Brody asked.

Agent G.B. smiled. "I want to welcome you!"

"Welcome us?" Sophia asked.

"Welcome you to the Secret Slide Money Club," Agent G.B. said. "I'm glad I rescued you from Albatross."

The three friends did not know what he was talking about.

"Albatross? Who's that?" Jake asked.

"Albatross wants to make everyone an Albie," Agent G.B. said.

The kids looked at each other. *An Albie?* (Say it with me: *AL-bee*.)

"Albies must do everything Albatross tells them to do," Agent G.B. said. "Albatross uses bad money choices to turn people into Albies."

"Money choices?" Brody asked.

"Yes," said Agent G.B. "The choices we make with money can be good or bad. Albatross can use bad money choices to make you his Albie."

"How do we know if someone is an Albie?" Sophia asked.

"They smell REALLY bad," Agent G.B. said.

"They smell bad? That's weird," Sophia said.

"It is weird. They smell like dirty, wet socks," Agent G.B. said.

"EWWWWWW!" Sophia said.

Brody laughed. "That is so funny!"

"Wait. We stink," Jake said.

The smell had started when they laughed about not giving to help the pet shelter. It must have been a bad money choice.

"Maybe giving is important," said Sophia. She stood quietly for a second. "Look, I can help the pet shelter."

"Me too," Brody said. "My mom gave me a dollar today."

"I get my allowance on Monday. I can chip in too," Jake said.

"You are lucky," Agent G.B. said. "I was able to get to you before Albatross. You were on the path to becoming Albies. And now I am giving you the chance to be Secret Slide Money Club agents."

Jake looked at his suit and tie. He and his friends *did* look like agents. "Well, that explains the clothes," he said.

"Um . . . do I really need a tie on my head for this?" Brody asked.

Agent G.B. looked at Brody. "Oh. Sorry about that. Looks like the slide needs a tune-up."

Brody sighed.

"What do the agents do?" Jake asked.

"Secret Slide Money Club agents help others avoid or fight Albatross."

"How do we rescue people from Albatross?" Jake asked.

Agent G.B. said, "They must follow the Master's Money Plan. It's simple. Give first. Then save some money. And then use what is left over for everything else."

"Give—Save—Live," said Sophia. "Like the buttons by the slide."

"Who is the Master?" Brody asked.

Agent G.B. smiled. "He knows everything about everything. He hates Albatross. You can trust His plan."

The three friends nodded.

"I saved you from Albatross so you could save others," Agent G.B. said.

"So how do we become agents?" Jake asked.

"You must complete three challenges," Agent G.B. said.

Jake, Sophia, and Brody looked at each other. They shrugged their shoulders.

"We'll give it a try," said Jake.

"Great," said Agent G.B. "Here is your first challenge: help Drew be generous. He wants to raise money for the pet shelter, but he doesn't know how."

A picture of Drew came up on the screen next to Agent G.B.

"Hey, we know Drew! He's in our class," said Sophia.

"Yes," said Agent G.B. "Drew has been worried that he won't have any money to give to the fund-raiser."

"So that's why he was sad," Brody said.

"Be careful," said Agent G.B. "Albatross hates generosity. He will try to stop Drew."

A verse went up on another screen. It said:

Each person should do as he has decided in his heart—not reluctantly or out of compulsion, since God loves a cheerful giver.—2 Corinthians 9:7

"Here is a verse for your mission. Give it to Drew," said Agent G.B.

Sophia wrote the verse in her notebook. "Got it!"

"Oh," Agent G.B. said. "Look in that backpack on the table."

Jake went over to the table. He opened the bag. Inside was something that looked like a jar. It said "GIVE" on it.

"That is your GIVE capsule," said Agent G.B. "Put Drew's money inside."

Brody went over to look at the rocket car.

"Do you want to drive it?" Agent G.B. asked.

"YES!" Brody said.

"Hop in," said Agent G.B.

Brody jumped in the car.

"You can get in too," Agent G.B. said to Jake and Sophia. "There are three seats."

"Brody driving a car?" Sophia asked.

Brody pressed a button. The rocket car started.

VROOOOOOM!

Chapter 4
Knock, Knock

Jake and Sophia got in the rocket car. It was a tight fit.

"Before you go, remember this—do not tell anyone your real identity," said Agent G.B.

"What are our secret agent names, then?" asked Sophia.

Agent G.B. smiled. "Agent Jake, Agent Sophia, and Agent Brody."

The three agents looked at each other. "Won't people figure it out?" Sophia asked.

"Not if you keep your really cool sunglasses on," said Agent G.B.

They looked at each other again. They were not sure if they believed their strange new friend.

"Really?" said Jake.

"Um . . . okay," said Sophia.

"Does my tie have to stay on my head?" Brody asked.

"For now," said Agent G.B.

Brody's tie kept covering his eyes. He tried to push it up, but it did not stay.

"Ugh," Brody said. "Someone hold my tie up while I drive."

Jake laughed. "No problem," he said.

Sophia looked up at a clock on the headquarters wall. It read 10:00.

"Hey, I need to be home at 12:00 for lunch," said Sophia.

"Me too," said Jake. "I will be grounded if I am late. We have two hours."

Brody pressed the car's pedal to the floor. *VROOOOOOM!* Flames came out of the rockets.

"Hold on!" yelled Brody.

The rocket car sped out of a secret door and out onto the street. Brody drove it around curve after curve. It was the fastest they had ever been.

SCREEEECH!

Brody slammed the brakes of the rocket car in front of Drew's house. The three agents hopped out.

"That was fast!" said Jake.

Sophia held her stomach. "I think I got carsick."

"Don't forget to wear your sunglasses," Jake said.

"Sunglasses on!" Brody said.

They walked onto the porch of Drew's house, and Sophia rang the doorbell.

Drew opened the door. "Um . . . yes?"

"Hi, Drew," said Jake. "I'm Agent Jake. This is Agent Sophia and Agent Brody."

Drew looked at the three agents. "You look familiar. Have we met before?"

The three friends looked at each other.

"Um . . . that's . . . um . . . funny," said Sophia. "We are here to help."

"With what?" asked Drew.

"You want to raise money for the pet shelter, right?" said Jake.

"How did you know that?" asked Drew.

"Don't worry about it," said Sophia. "We know you are bummed."

Drew looked down. "I don't have any money to give. Our class needs twenty dollars to hit our goal," said Drew.

"I think I know how to get twenty dollars," said Jake.

"How?" asked Drew.

Jake smiled. "Do you like lemonade?"

"Of course. Everyone does. My mom just bought a bunch of lemons for lemonade," said Drew.

"Perfect," said Jake.

Sophia remembered the buttons next to the slide. "Give—Save—Live," she said. "Giving is the first and most important thing we do with money."

"What?" said Drew.

"If Albatross hates good money choices, then he will really hate this," said Sophia.

"You are right," said Jake. "We need to be careful."

Jake opened the backpack and took out the GIVE capsule.

"This is your GIVE capsule," Jake said to Drew. "It's where we will put the money."

Drew looked at Brody. "Why is your tie on your head?"

Brody shook his head. "You would not believe me if I told you."

Jake and Sophia chuckled.

"You know, you all kind of stink," Drew said. He wrinkled his nose.

"I know," Sophia said. "We are working on it."

Come on," Jake said. "Let's help Drew sell some lemonade!"

Chapter 5

Lemons on the Loose

Brody walked into Drew's kitchen, holding a lot of lemons. "I've got the lemons!"

"Be careful, Brody," said Sophia. "The floor is wet. We spilled some water."

"No problem!" said Brody. "I would never fall!"

Brody started to show off by dancing. But when he tried to spin around, his tie covered his eyes. He couldn't see.

Brody's foot hit some water on the floor. His leg went up in the air. So did the lemons.

"WHOOOOOOA!" yelled Brody.

"LOOK OUT!" yelled Sophia.

It was too late. Lemons were flying everywhere.

Brody fell to the floor and landed on a lemon. Lemon juice squirted up in the air and landed behind his glasses.

"AAAAAAAAH!" yelled Brody. "My eye! My eye! It burns!"

Sophia ran over to help. But she slipped on one of the lemons too.

Jake heard the crash and ran into the kitchen. He slipped on a lemon and fell too! The three friends were on the floor.

Drew looked in the kitchen. "What kind of agents are you?"

"Wet and sticky ones," said Brody.

They picked up the mess. "We need to hurry if we are going to raise twenty dollars before lunch," said Jake.

Sophia went to go make a sign. She wrote, *LEMONADE! 50¢ per cup.* "So, how many cups do we need to sell?" she said.

Sophia pulled out her notebook. For every two cups they sold, they would get a dollar. She wrote,

$$50¢ + 50¢ = \$1.00$$

So how many cups would they need to sell? She wrote,

$$20 \text{ dollars} \times 2 \text{ cups per dollar} = 40 \text{ cups}$$

So they needed to sell forty cups to get twenty dollars. "Um, Jake and Brody?" she said.

Jake and Brody looked up.

"We need to sell forty cups of lemonade," said Sophia.

"Wow. That's a lot of lemonade," said Jake.

"Yikes. And we really need to hurry. It's 10:30," Brody said.

"I'll set up a table outside," said Jake. "You two start squeezing lemons."

Jake went outside. He set up the table in Drew's front yard.

"This will be a great spot," Jake said to himself.

Just as he finished, he saw something strange. Another table was being set up across the street. And two kids put lemonade on it!

Jake looked over at them. They looked back at him with angry faces. Who were they?

Then, Jake smelled something. "Ugh! What is that smell? It smells like . . . like . . . dirty . . . wet . . . socks."

CHALLENGE BREAK!

Whew! You finished five chapters. Only five more chapters left.

This is a good time to get up, stretch, and say the alphabet backwards.

Ready? Z, Y, X, W, V . . .

Just kidding. You don't need to do that.

But we can learn some cool things about money. Let me give you three facts.

Fact #1: Dollar bills are not made of paper. They are made of cotton and linen (like your clothes!).

Fact #2: In 1934 (a long time ago), the United States made $100,000 bills. One bill for $100,000! I would hate to lose that one. Yikes!

Fact #3: There are 119 grooves on the side of a quarter. Check it out. Pretty groovy!

Cool, right?

Okay. Let's get back to the story. I hope Jake, Sophia, and Brody can help Drew get that twenty dollars. It would stink if they failed their first challenge.

Chapter 6

Friends Versus Smelly Guys

Sophia, Brody, and Drew came outside with the lemonade, the sign, and extra lemons.

"Hey, what are they doing?" yelled Sophia.

"Smell that?" asked Jake. "They must be some of Albatross's Albies."

"EWWWWW! Dirty, wet socks." Brody pinched his nose. "They smell worse than we do!"

Drew looked across the street. "Why are they selling lemonade too?"

"They don't want you to reach your goal. They are trying to stop your giving," said Jake.

"Why?" said Drew.

"Because giving is the most powerful thing you can do with money," Sophia said. "And when you give, it means you are *not* following Albatross."

"Right," Jake said. "He's a bad dude."

"And he stinks!" Brody said.

The two Albies looked over at Sophia's sign. Then they wrote *Only 25¢ per cup!* on their sign.

"Look!" said Sophia. "Their lemonade costs less."

Sophia thought for a second. She wrote in her notebook:

$$25¢ + 25¢ + 25¢ + 25¢ = \$1$$

"If each cup costs twenty-five cents, we need four cups to earn one dollar," said Sophia.

Sophia did some math in her notebook.

$$\textit{4 cups per dollar x \$20 = 80 cups}$$

"We would have to sell eighty cups to reach our goal!" Sophia yelled.

A line of people started to form at the Albies' stand. Nobody was going over to Drew's stand.

The two Albies pointed at Brody's head and began to laugh.

"They are making fun of my tie!" said Brody. "Now we really have to beat them!"

"Well, it is funny." Sophia snickered.

"Come on. Let's lower our price," Jake said.

They marked out the *50¢* and put *25¢*. Some people started coming over to their stand.

"It's working," said Brody.

"We still need more people!" said Sophia.

Brody started yelling, "Lemonade! Get your fresh lemonade here! Only 25¢!"

More people got in line.

But as Brody yelled, a lemon hit him.

"OUCH!!!" yelled Brody.

Then another lemon hit him. "HEY!!!"

Brody looked across the street. He could not believe what he saw.

"LOOK OUT, AGENTS!!!" yelled Brody.

The great lemonade-stand standoff had begun.

Chapter 7
Take Cover!

"Uh-oh. Where did they get *that*?" said Sophia.

The Albies were putting a bunch of lemons into a catapult. They were going to launch the lemons at the agents.

"TAKE COVER!!!" yelled Jake.

The catapult threw the lemons in the air. Drew and the agents dove under the stand. Lemons hit the table, cups, and lemonade.

The people in line ran away.

"They are destroying our stand!" said Brody.

"And scaring our customers!" said Sophia.

Jake stuck his head out from the stand. He looked across the street. The Albies were going to launch more lemons.

"STAY DOWN!!!" he yelled.

Lemon grenades were everywhere! They slammed the stand. They sunk the sign. They crushed the cups.

"Quick! Grab some lemons!" said Jake.

Jake and Sophia picked up a few lemons from the ground. Drew handed Brody a water blaster.

"Where did you get this?" asked Brody.

"I keep it around," said Drew with a shrug.

Brody filled the water blaster up with lemonade.

"LET'S GET THEM!!!" yelled Jake.

Jake and Sophia threw lemons at the Albies. Brody squirted one of the Albies with lemonade. Some went in his eye. The Albie yelled and ran away.

"I know how it feels!" said Brody.

Sophia hit the other Albie in the arm with half a lemon. That Albie ran away too.

"Got him!" Sophia yelled.

Then it stopped. Everything was quiet.

"They won't bother us anymore," Jake said.

They looked at Drew. He still was sad. They looked at the lemonade stand. It was a mess.

"It's ruined!" said Sophia.

Their lemonade was spilled. Cups were everywhere. Their sign had a hole in it.

"They destroyed our stand and scared everyone away," said Brody.

Next to the stand was the last of the lemonade.

"We still have some lemonade left," said Jake.

Drew looked at Jake. "No. It's over. We will not be able to raise the money now."

It was 11:00. The agents were sad. They felt like they had failed their first challenge.

"We need to be back home in one hour," said Jake. "Agent G.B. won't be happy."

"So much for being Secret Slide Money Club agents," said Sophia.

They were quiet.

Then Brody looked over at the rocket car. "Drew, do you have a wagon?"

"Yes," said Drew. "Why?"

Brody smiled. "I have an idea."

Jake and Sophia looked at each other. They had no idea what would happen next.

Chapter 8
A Tie-riffic Idea

"How many more cups of lemonade do we need to sell?" asked Brody.

Sophia looked at the GIVE capsule. They had five dollars in it. She took out her notebook and did the math:

$$\$20 - \$5 = \$15$$

"Remember, if each cup costs twenty-five cents, we need four cups to get one dollar. So four times fifteen dollars equals sixty cups."

She showed Jake and Brody her notebook:

$$\$15 \times 4 \text{ cups per dollar} = 60 \text{ cups}$$

"We can't do it," said Jake. "No one is around. The Albies scared everyone away."

"We *can* do it. We can find more people," said Brody, moving the tie out of his eyes once again.

"There isn't enough time," said Sophia. "We would need to go really fast."

"Oh, we can go fast," Brody said. "Drew, get your wagon."

Drew brought out his wagon. Brody put the wagon behind the rocket car. He took the tie off his head.

"I knew this would come in handy," Brody said.

Brody used his tie to connect the rocket car and the wagon. He grinned.

"All right!" said Brody. "Get the cups and lemonade and put them in the wagon. Someone needs to hold them while I drive."

Jake and Sophia looked at each other. "I don't think he's joking," Jake said.

"I don't know if I like this idea," said Sophia.

Jake let Drew and Sophia get in the car. He got in the wagon.

"I got this!" said Jake.

Jake held the cups and the lemonade. Brody jumped in the car and pushed the start button.

VROOOOM!

"Hold on!" Brody yelled.

Chapter 9
Goal!

The rocket car sped down the road. Jake held on to the wagon and the lemonade.

"YIKES!!!" said Sophia. The rocket car went around a turn. She looked back at Jake. He had almost lost the lemonade.

SCREEECH!!!

Brody stopped the rocket car next to a soccer field. A lot of people were watching a game on the field.

Brody got out of the car. "This spot should work."

"Great idea," said Jake. "If there is one thing I know about soccer, it's that it makes you really thirsty! Let's sell some lemonade!"

The friends and Drew started yelling. "Lemonade! Lemonade! Get your fresh lemonade!"

People heard them and started walking over. The people bought lemonade for themselves and their friends.

"Great idea, Brody!" Sophia said.

"And good use of your tie!" Jake said.

The crowd grew and grew. The friends filled up cups fast. They sold a lot of lemonade.

Just then, Sophia froze. "Hey, do you smell that? Dirty, wet socks. Gross!"

Jake smelled the air. "You are right. The Albies must be around here somewhere."

Jake spotted the Albies who had messed up the lemonade stand walking by. He ran after them. "Stop!"

The Albies turned around.

"Why are you trying to stop us from following the Master's Money Plan?" Jake asked.

"We do what Albatross tells us to do," one said. "And he hates when people use money to help others."

"Why are you his Albies?" asked Jake.

"We made some bad money decisions," the Albie said. "And now we must do what Albatross wants us to do."

Jake saw that the Albies were wearing bracelets. Suddenly the bracelets started to glow red, and the Albies ran away.

"Wait!" Jake yelled. "We can help you!"

The Albies kept running. They never looked back.

Sophia and Brody caught up with Jake. They were holding the GIVE capsule.

"Look, Jake!" Sophia said. "We raised a lot of money for Drew!"

Sophia showed Jake the money. There were fifteen dollars.

"We have to go," Jake said. "Let's take Drew home and then get back to headquarters."

They got into the rocket car and sped off to Drew's house.

When they arrived, Drew jumped out of the car.

"Here is your wagon," Jake said. "Wow! That was a fun ride!"

Sophia handed Drew the GIVE capsule.

"And here is fifteen dollars!" Sophia said.

Drew was glad. "Thank you so much!" he said.

"Happy to help!" Brody said.

"I just wish we had five dollars more to reach the goal," Drew said.

The three friends looked at each other and smiled.

"Don't worry, Drew," Jake said. "I'm sure some of your classmates will give to the pet shelter on Monday."

"Your class will reach the goal," Brody said with a smile. "I promise."

"Giving is not only fun, but it can also help others," said Sophia. "That's the Master's Plan. Give—Save—Live."

Jake thought for a second. He smiled. "Giving is the first thing we should do with money!" he said.

"Imagine what could happen if we all did that," Brody said.

Drew looked at his watch. "Hey, don't you need to get back?"

"He's right," said Jake. "Let's go."

Sophia remembered the mission's verse. "Wait!" she said. She ripped the page out of her notebook and gave it to Drew.

"Read it," yelled Sophia as she ran back to the rocket car.

Drew read the verse:

Each person should do as he has decided in his heart—not reluctantly or out of compulsion, since God loves a cheerful giver.—2 Corinthians 9:7

"Thanks!" said Drew. "I am very cheerful about giving this money! I am so glad I get to help the pet shelter!"

"We know," said Sophia. "We're happy for you."

The three friends jumped into the rocket car. Brody pressed the pedal. *VROOOOM!*

Chapter 10

One Down, Two More to Go

Jake, Sophia, and Brody were back at headquarters. The computers and buttons were flashing and beeping. Agent G.B. was on the big screen.

"Well done!" he said. "You finished your first challenge."

"Whew! It wasn't easy," said Jake.

"You were right about Albatross," said Sophia. "He sent two of his Albies to stop us."

"I thought he would," said Agent G.B.

"The Albies had bracelets on," said Jake. "They ran away when the bracelets started glowing red."

"Ah, yes," said Agent G.B. "That is how Albatross contacts them. He must be trying to get more Albies."

"It can't be fun to be an Albie," said Brody. "You smell bad and have to do everything Albatross says."

"Oh, it isn't fun," said Agent G.B. "That is why we need Secret Slide Money Club agents. To help people avoid becoming Albies."

Jake smelled his shirt. He did not stink anymore. Helping the class reach their goal took away the bad smell.

Brody walked over to a round table. On the table were three watches. The watches had screens on them.

"Cool!" said Brody. "Are these for us?"

"They are," said Agent G.B. "Take one."

Jake, Sophia, and Brody each put a watch on their wrists.

"These watches will let me contact you," said Agent G.B. "You can also use them to call each other."

Brody chuckled. "Can we use them during class?"

Sophia gave Brody a frustrated look. "No. Do not get me in any more trouble!"

Jake and Brody smiled. "We would never do that. . . ."

Agent G.B. looked at Brody. There was something missing.

"Brody, where is your tie?" asked Agent G.B.

Brody didn't say anything. He reached into his pocket and pulled out a really dirty, stretched tie.

"Um . . . did you know that this tie can pull a wagon behind the rocket car?" said Brody.

Agent G.B. shook his head.

"I'm glad it came in handy," he said. "Hey, don't you have to get home?"

The three looked at their watches. It was 11:55. They only had five minutes to get home!

"Uh-oh!" said Sophia. "We need to hurry! How do we get our normal clothes?"

Agent G.B. smiled and nodded his head to the left. "That elevator will take you to a secret door on the big playground rock. When you step out—you'll be yourselves again."

"Wow. That's cool," Jake said.

Jake and Sophia saw that Brody was chewing something. They did not say anything. They just looked at Brody.

"Oh," said Brody. "I found it under that table. Tastes like mint!"

Jake and Sophia were grossed out. But they had to leave. The three friends said goodbye to Agent G.B. and headed home.

The first challenge was a success. But they needed to complete two more challenges to become agents. And the next one would be a Mad Cash Dash!

Your Money Challenge

Wait! Wait! Wait! Before you close the book, I have something for you.

Jake, Sophia, and Brody are not the only ones who get a challenge in this book. You do too!

Secret Slide Money Club agents are generous. They follow the Master's Money Plan: Give—Save—Live. Now is your chance to act like an agent.

So here is your Money Challenge. . . .

Give something away. It can be money. But it does not have to be.

Here are a few ideas:

- Give money to your church this week.

- Give a book to your library.
- Share your snack with a friend.

Or come up with your own idea. Just go and give. You can do it. I know you can.

See you in the next book! And please don't chew old gum, like Brody. Yuck!

(Okay. Now you can close the book.)

**Keep reading for a sneak peek
at book 2 . . .**

Le Bowl of Chocolate Rock Starz

BOOM!" Jake yelled. He raised his arms up. He was still holding his paintbrush. "I am the painting champion!"

Jake, Sophia, and Brody were in art class. The art teacher had let them paint whatever they wanted. Sophia looked over at Jake's painting.

"Not bad . . . I think," Sophia said. "What is it?"

Jake put down his arms. He was shocked.

"What do you mean?" he said. "It's Henry Gold hitting a home run! He's the best baseball player ever!"

Sophia squinted. "It looks like a fish. Are you sure you didn't paint a fish?"

Jake gave Sophia an angry look. "It's not a fish."

Sophia laughed.

"Well, what did *you* paint?" Jake asked Sophia. He crossed his arms.

"The Mona Lisa," Sophia said. Sophia showed her painting to Jake. The teacher came over to see it.

"Oh my!" the art teacher said. "That is amazing! It looks so much like the real Mona Lisa. Great job, Sophia!"

The teacher walked away. Jake rolled his eyes.

Brody was working hard on his painting. He didn't even notice Jake and Sophia looking over his shoulder.

"What are you painting?" Jake asked.

Brody jumped. "Yikes! Don't scare me like that! You could make me mess up."

Sophia looked at Brody's painting. "Is that . . . umm . . . a bowl of cereal?"

"You got it!" said Brody. "I call this . . . *Le Bowl of Chocolate Rock Starz.*"

"*Le?*" asked Jake.

"Do you like it? It sounds fancy." Brody smiled.

"It's actually not bad . . . for a bowl of cereal," Sophia said.

"Mmm. A bowl of cereal sounds good right now," Brody said, licking his lips.

"EWWW! You are drooling, Brody!" Sophia said.

Brody laughed. He wiped his mouth.

Jake held out his arms, trying to get Sophia and Brody quiet.

"Hey, do you smell that?" he said. "It smells like . . . dirty . . . wet . . . socks!"

Jake, Sophia, and Brody held their noses.

Just then their classmate Kate walked over. She looked different today. She wasn't smiling and smelled really bad, like an Albie.

"Hey, look what I painted," said Kate. It's my favorite toy, a Pretty and Plush Pony. I love Pretty and Plush Ponies."

"Oh, that's cool," Jake said. He was still holding his nose.

Brody was covering his mouth and snickering. Jake and Sophia turned to Brody.

"What's so funny, Brody?" Sophia asked.

Brody started laughing and pointing at the painting. "She likes PRETTY AND PLUSH PONIES!!! Those are for little kids!"

Jake and Sophia were not laughing. Both had their arms crossed.

"Don't make fun of her," Sophia said. "We all like different toys."

"Yeah. Don't you have a lot of Sammy the Snuggly Snails in your room?" asked Jake.

Brody stopped laughing. His face turned red.

"Um . . . maybe," Brody said. "The box says *For Ages 2+*. I'm a plus."

"It's okay for you to like Sammy the Snuggly Snails," Sophia said. "And it's also okay for Kate to like Pretty and Plush Ponies."

"But I also have some really cool video games," Brody said.

Jake and Sophia shook their heads.

Kate looked at the three friends. "Well, I am going to buy more ponies. I must get them all."

"But there are more than a hundred Pretty and Plush Ponies," said Brody.

"I know. And I will get them all. Every time I get paid for my chores, I buy more ponies," said Kate.

"Yikes. Where do you keep them all?" asked Sophia.

Kate looked down. "I want a Pretty and Plush Barn for my ponies. But it costs $35.00. I never have enough money to buy it."

Sophia smiled. "You should save your money for it!"

Kate shook her head and walked away. "No saving for me! Spend—Spend—Spend! I love to spend!"

Just then, the three friends' watches made a pinging sound. Agent G.B. needed them at the headquarters after school.

"Yes!" Jake said. A new challenge.

The three friends needed to complete three challenges to become Secret Slide Money Club agents. They were excited to get a new one.

Sophia took out her notebook and wrote,

Spend—Spend—Spend?
Kate does not save any money.
And Kate smells like an Albie.

They looked across the art room at Kate. They had a feeling they knew what their next challenge would be.

About the Author

Art Rainer is an Albatross fighter. He helps people make good money choices (Give—Save—Live) so they will not become smelly, mean Albies. Art is the author of *The Money Challenge: 30 Days of Discovering God's Design for You and Your Money*. He is married to Sarah and has three sons—Nathaniel, Joshua, and James.